Fishfingers Fred, the art thief, has been spotted in the area.

The police cats are going to the City Art Gallery to keep watch.

Constable Kitt gets in and puts on her seat belt.
Police Car's powerful engine **roars** into life.

On the way, Sergeant Mogg tells Constable Kitt about
Fishfingers Fred. He only steals paintings of **fish**.

Police Car
on Patrol

Peter Bently

Illustrated by Martha Lightfoot

NEW
BURLINGTON
BOOKS

Constable Kitt is getting Police Car ready for **night patrol.**

Sergeant Mogg receives an **alert.**

There is a **famous** painting of some fish at the City Art Gallery.

Police Car soon reaches the gallery.

Constable Kitt turns off the lights and parks down a side street opposite the gallery.

Suddenly,
they see someone
climbing out of a
window, carrying
something large and
wearing a mask.

Constable Kitt
turns on Police
Car's extra-bright
headlights.

"Stop! Police!"
booms Sergeant Mogg.

The thief **runs away** from the police cats,
quickly climbs into a getaway car...

...and **speeds** off!

NEE-NAW
NEE-NAW!

Sergeant Mogg switches on Police Car's siren and flashing lights.

Police Car **chases**
after the thief.

POLICE

Z000M!

Sergeant Mogg
radioes for back-up.

They **speed** around corners and **whizz** down empty streets.

The thief is fast, but Constable Kitt has had special training and can drive **quickly** and **safely**.

The police cats follow
the thief to a dark and twisty lane.

CHUCKA!

CHUCKA!

They lose sight of
the getaway car.

A police
helicopter
hovers
overhead.

The pilot **radioes** Police Car. "I've got the thief in my searchlight! He's turning north."

They head north into a forest but the trees block the pilot's view. Then Constable Kitt spots a track with **fresh tyre marks!**

At the end of the track is a **dark hut.** Constable Kitt switches off Police Car's lights.

Sergeant Mogg agrees to go round the back while Constable Kitt goes in the front.

Sergeant Mogg **slips** around the side of the hut.
"Now!" he whispers into his walkie-talkie.

Constable Kitt **forces open** the front door.

The thief runs
out the back.
But Sergeant Mogg
is **waiting!**

Sergeant Mogg pulls the mask off the thief.
It's Fishfingers Fred!

"You're under arrest," Sergeant Mogg says.
He puts handcuffs on Fishfingers Fred.

The **back-up** vehicles have arrived.
Fishfingers Fred is shut inside the police van.

"**Congratulations, Officers,**"
says the Superintendent. "Now we can return
the paintings so **everyone** can enjoy them!"

"Thank you," says Sergeant Mogg.
"But we couldn't have done it without Police Car!"

Let's look at
Police Car

Speaker

Two-way
radio

Powerful
engine

Extra-bright
headlights

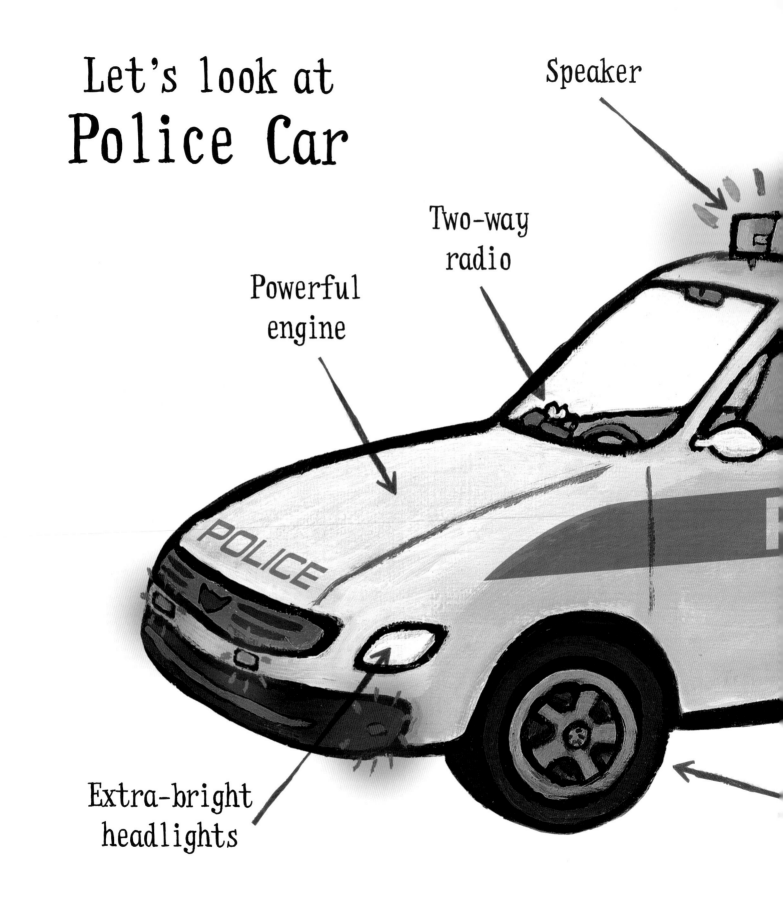